To: Grandma
& the grandchildren
to read together. Enjoy!

Andrea M Burris

2010

A Dog Lover's

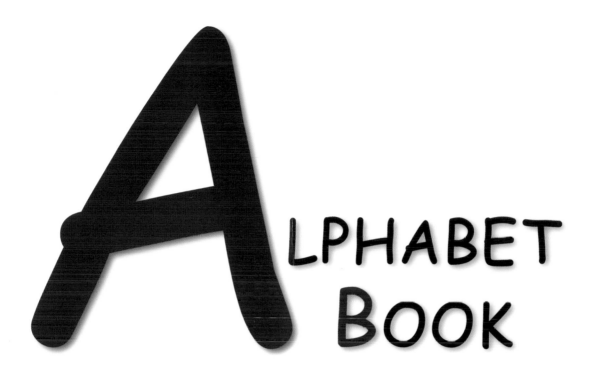

Alphabet Book

ANDREA BURRIS & ANNA SCHAD

ILLUSTRATED BY ANDREA BURRIS

A special pat on the head and scratch behind the ears for our kids, Matt, Stuart, Charlie, Keith, Frank and Joel who remind us that play is an important part of everyone's day. And an <u>extra</u> special kibble for David Burris and Scott Schad for crisis management and moral support in the line of duty.

--Andrea Burris and Anna Schad--

Library of Congress Control Number: 2007903502

For information or orders contact:
A & D Books, Inc. 5096 E. 400, Big Cabin, OK 74332
Tel: (918) 785-5779

Published by:
A & D Books, Inc.
5096 E. 400
Big Cabin, OK 74332
Tel: (918) 785-5779

Prepared by:
Stuart M. Ryan

Printed and bound in china

A Dog Lover's Alphabet Book
ISBN: 9780974329413   US $14.95   CANADA $19.95

An Airedale named Almost always arrives
To eat from his dish at a quarter 'til five.
As amazing a thing as ever you've seen,
Almost always licks the bowl clean.

GRRRRR—

Bulldog, boxer and beagle,

Each on a leash to stay legal,

Tie their owners in knots, as they go on their trots

Then low-five each other and "geegle."

C is for Carson who loves to chew,

Gnawing and nibbling as puppies do!

Furniture and pillows, all have such appeal.

Perhaps the next chair should be made out of steel!

Dale loves his dog house, his private domain,
A diligent vigil he's forced to maintain.
Came a curious cat and his kitty-cat crowd,
Dale put up his sign. It reads "No Cats Allowed!"

Edsel enjoys going out for a drive.

With the wind in his face, he feels so alive.

Edsel loves steering, if only he could.

The question is whether you think that he should?!

Fred flung the Frisbee with awesome force,

But it went too high, and a little off course.

Intended for Freckles, it seems so unfair,

That Fran jumped in front and caught it mid-air.

reat gobs of garbage fell off of the truck,

A great and yet glorious can full of yuck!

The two had been sniffing for something to eat.

Gus dove in head first, Gavin jumped to his feet,

That rock the truck struck on the side of the street

Must have been lucky! We're talking sweet!"

Having a hound dog like Hector around
Brought us closer to all of our neighbors, we've found.
The noise from his howling, the "Hectorious" din,
We return all the news, shoes, and balls that fly in!

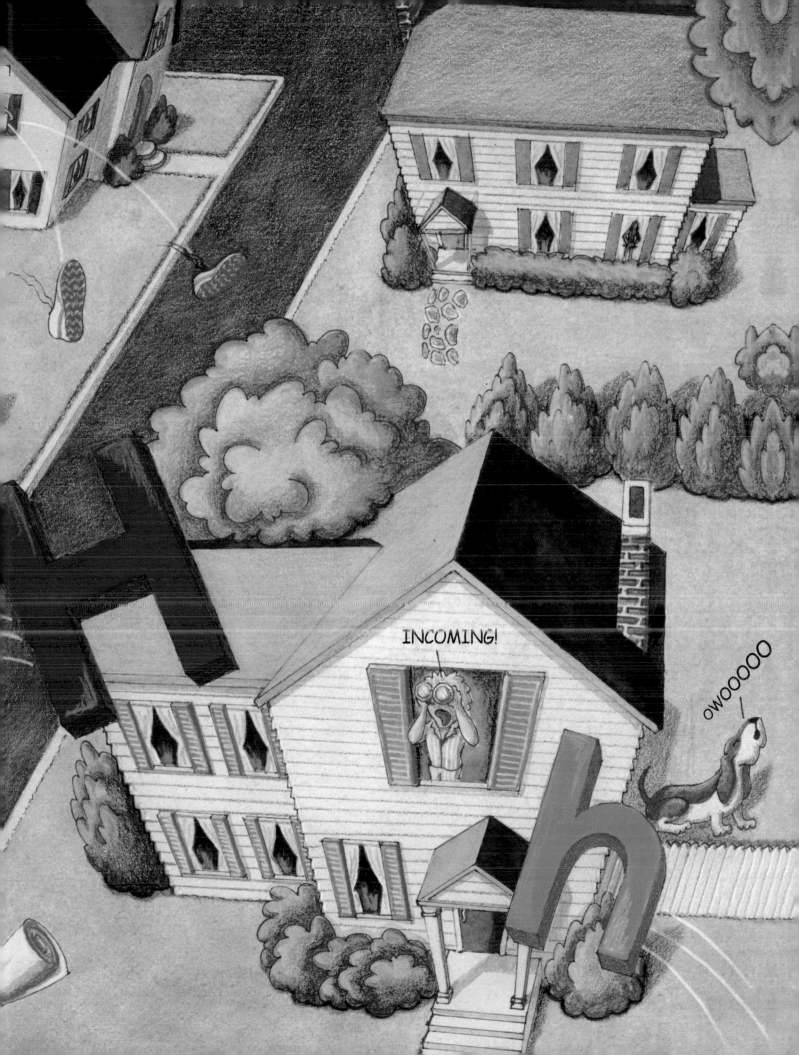

I van was itching before anyone knew it.

First a scratch here and there, then he really went to it.

It isn't as if there's no reason to twitch.

A circus of fleas would make anyone itch!

J ustin walked in just as Jasper jumped back.
He'd jimmied the lock in search of a snack.
Justin keeps Jasper's food locked up at night,
'cause Jasper just has to sneak in for a "bite".

K is for Kelso, it's 5:45.

He's landed on Kip with a perfect swan dive.

Eager to play, he means Kip no harm,

But with Kelso around, who needs an alarm?!

Luke leaped and lunged from side to side,

He languished on his leash.

The fire hydrant just ahead was clearly out of reach.

The cat, the squirrel, the postman too,

   would never be attained.

Nothing makes a dog more blue than knowing he's restrained!

Marshall's Meat Market only sells meat.
Considered by many the finest to eat,
Ham, links and sausage all hung with such care,
Mark, Matt, and Max think "How thoughtful to share!"

N is for never, "Are you listening, young man?!

"We've been down that puppy road time and again!"

"The piddling, the chewing, the whining at night!"

"We'll take the floppy-eared one on the right."

O is for Ogden who loves to go out,
Digging and playing and romping about.
So you clean the floors, but you can't win
When Ogden brings the outside in!

P ete is protective but always polite.

Not that he isn't itching to bite.

Don't step out of line, Pete's poised and ready.

Sometimes it's hard to hold your cup steady!

Quinn looks with a question, then quivers and quakes.

No doubt the direction the car's going to take.

It's off to the vet and all that implies.

You can tell by the panicked look in his eyes!

Rascal ran out when I opened the door.
Retrieving's his game, he's done this before!
Our porch overflowing with all he collects,
We only hope none of the neighbors suspect!

S is for shedding, Spring's annual curse.

First a hair here and there, then it quickly got worse!

Steve, armed with his shop vac made his last stand.

He went right to the source and sucked every last strand!

Tommy's in trouble, he stumbled, he fell.

He calls out for Laddie, he's down in a well.

Laddie comes running hearing his yell,

Then quick as a wink he calls on his cell.

Ulysses is a bloodhound, his fate unsure,

His talent unusual, his gift obscure.

Forgetting his training, his future's forsaken.

Ulysses is happy to just sniff out bacon!

Victor was vexed, there's no question of that.

It's always the same with the neighbors darn cat.

The cat sneaks up softly, first a scratch, then a screech!

The he jumps on the fence overhead out of reach!

When it comes to the water, they can't get enough.

Living with dogs such as these can be rough!

A warning to owners who have such a pet,

Know that you're going to get wetter than wet!

Xavier, the famous X-ray dog was very smart indeed.
He studied hard in doggy school, in fact he was degreed.
Quite the expert in his field, and that's a well-known fact.
Imagine our extreme dismay, he X-rayed our poor cat!

Yvette and Yvonne were quite a pair,

With yellow ribbons in their hair.

They'd yip and yap of styles and such,

As if it really mattered much.

How funny that they each prefer

The tresses of the other her.

Zounds! How Zippy loves to run.

He zips, he zings! It must be fun!

Zippy has zoomed since the day he was born,

Which explains why the rugs in the house are so worn!